Counting on the Woods

to the waterfall
given for all

In memory of Kathleen and Dodo,
and for the woods they loved.
—G.E.L.

For friends and neighbors in Elliott County,
this treasured Appalachian home we share.
—A.W.O.

Counting on the Woods

a poem by George Ella Lyon
photographs by Ann W. Olson

A DK INK BOOK
DK PUBLISHING, INC.

One path,

a stick for a staff.

Two birds,

daybreak's words.

*Mourning doves perched
in a black walnut tree*

Hercules beetle, stag beetle and spotted grape beetle

Three bugs

in the moss rug.

Rye

Four worms,

    how the earth turns.

Five nests

Acadian flycatcher and nest

Bald-faced hornet nest

top, Broad-winged hawk nest
above, Tent caterpillar nest
left, Eastern bluebird and nest

where new ones rest.

Red–winged blackbird nest

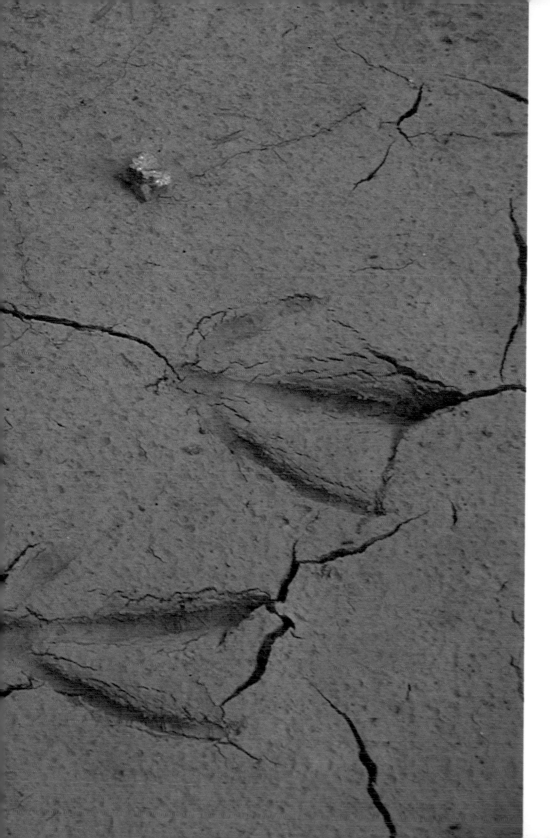

Six tracks.

Who's coming back?

Canada geese

Seven stones,

   the little creek's home.

Two crested dwarf iris with a star chickweed

Eight flowers

Three great trillium

fed on dirt

and showers.

Two pink lady's slippers

Nine vines,

earth to sky they climb.

Grape vines

Ten

trees

Sycamore tree

whose innumerable leaves

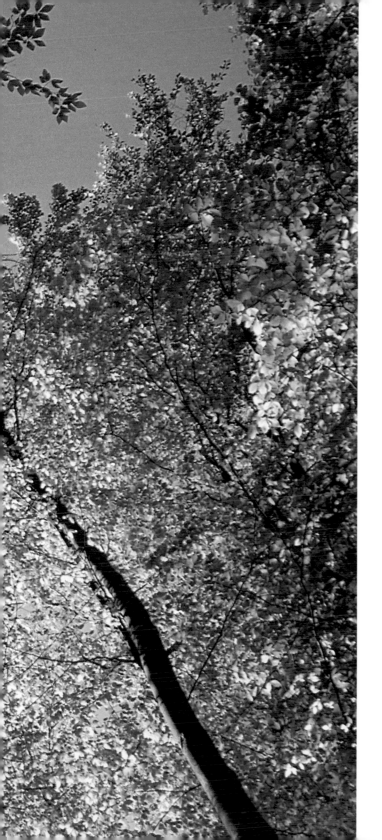

clean the air

for everything

that breathes.

Photo by Eric R. Olson

Photographer's acknowledgments: A photographer presses the shutter button alone but does better work with a wide range of assistance. I am deeply grateful to the following haulers, helpers, and scouts: Frank Olson, Eric and Rebecca Olson; Kyle McDaniel; George Plage, Sonata Bohen, and their daughters, Anna and Rosa; Dail, Ethel, and Joy Howard; Ellie Reser; Fred M. Busroe; Ed Scott; Ann Scott, Jennifer Scott, and Hanna Kjellen; Rebecca Greene; Carolyn Franzini; Charlie and Thelma Harris; Ken Sexton; Fred Howes; Wendy Fidao; Emily Norland; and Maura Carew.

I greatly appreciate the generosity of Richard Jackson, Jennifer Browne, John Flavell, J. Michael Phelps, Jr., MD, James Archambeault, entomologist A. Jonathan Smith, MD, Allen Perkins, Mike Hearn, John MacGregor, Tom Biebighauser, Steve Bonney, Elaine Conley, the fine folks at the Film Lab in Lexington, and of course Marie Bradby, Leatha Kendrick, Lou Martin, Jan Walters-Cook, and George Ella Lyon, with her gift of words to us all.

I took these photographs in eastern Kentucky, most of them near where I live in Elliott County. The Canada geese are found in nearby Rowan County at the Minor E. Clark State Fish Hatchery and at Cave Run Lake.

A Richard Jackson Book

DK Publishing, Inc
95 Madison Avenue
New York, NY 10016
Visit us on the World Wide Web at http://www.dk.com
Text copyright © 1998 by George Ella Lyon.
Photographs copyright © 1998 by Ann W. Olson.
Library of Congress Cataloging-in-Publication Data
Lyon, George Ella [date]
Counting on the woods / by George Ella Lyon ; photographs by Ann W. Olson. — 1st Edition.
p.   cm.
Summary: Uses rhyme to enumerate and describe natural objects seen while walking through the woods.
ISBN 0-7894-2480-0
1. Counting—Juvenile literature. 2. Forests and forestry—Kentucky—Pictorial works—Juvenile literature. [1. Counting. 2. Forests and forestry.] I. Olson, Ann W., ill. II. Title.
QA113.L97 1998 97-34117 513.2'11—dc21 CIP AC
The text of this book is set in 34 point Caslon.
Printed and bound in the United States of America.
First Edition, 1998
10 9 8 7 6 5 4 3 2

on the title page spread:
top left, Fowler's toad
bottom, Woodland snail
right, Worm-eating warbler